# A NOTE TO

Congratulations on choosing the best in educational materials for your child. By selecting top-quality McGraw-Hill products, you can be assured that the concepts used in our books will reinforce and enhance the skills that are being taught in classrooms nationwide.

And what better way to get young readers excited than with Mercer Mayer's Little Critter, a character loved by children everywhere? Our First Readers offer simple and engaging stories about Little Critter that children can read on their own. Each level incorporates reading skills, colorful illustrations, and challenging activities.

**Level 1** – The stories are simple and use repetitive language. Illustrations are highly supportive.

**Level 2** - The stories begin to grow in complexity. Language is still repetitive, but it is mixed with more challenging vocabulary.

**Level 3** - The stories are more complex. Sentences are longer and more varied.

To help your child make the most of this book, look at the first few pictures in the story and discuss what is happening. Ask your child to predict where the story is going. Then, once your child has read the story, have him or her review the word list and do the activities. This will reinforce vocabulary words from the story and build reading comprehension.

You are your child's first and most influential teacher. No one knows your child the way you do. Tailor your time together to reinforce a newly acquired skill or to overcome a temporary stumbling block. Praise your child's progress and ideas, take delight in his or her imagination, and most of all, enjoy your time together!

**McGraw-Hill
Children's Publishing**

Send all inquiries to:
McGraw-Hill Children's Publishing
8787 Orion Place
Columbus, OH 43240-4027

Printed in the United States of America.

1-57768-844-9

 A Big Tuna Trading Company, LLC/J. R. Sansevere Book

Library of Congress Cataloging-in-Publication Data is on file with the publisher.

1 2 3 4 5 6 7 8 9 10 PHXBK 07 06 05 04 03 02

*The McGraw-Hill Companies*

# FIRST READERS

Level 1   Grades PreK–K

# BEACH DAY

## by Mercer Mayer

Mc Graw Hill **McGraw-Hill**
**Children's Publishing**

Columbus, Ohio

4

We are going to the beach
with Dad today.
Hooray!

5

We spread out our towels.

# We swim with flippers.

# Word List

Read each word in the lists below. Then, find each word in the story. Now, make up a new sentence using the word. Say your sentence out loud.

| Words I Know | Challenge Words |
|---|---|
| we | build |
| beach | sandcastle |
| Dad | seashells |
| | almost |

# Matching Pictures

In each row, point to the picture that is the same as the first picture in the row.

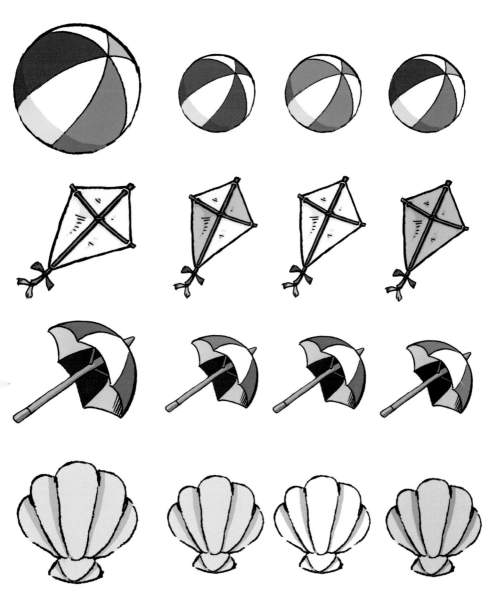

# Color Words

Look at each picture. Then, point to the color words that you would use to describe the picture.

 yellow   green   **pink**

 gray   white   purple

 orange   **blue**   yellow

 green   red   **blue**

# Understanding the Story

Answer the questions below. Point to the correct answer in each row. Try not to look back at the story.

Besides Dad, who went to the beach with Little Critter?

What was one of the things Little Critter did with Little Sister?

What did Little Critter almost take home with him?

# First Letter of a Word

Read each word. Then, point to the first letter of each word. Say the sound of the first letter out loud.

kite

ball

pail

fish

seashell

dune

# Action Words

Action words tell what is happening in a story.

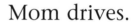

Example:
Little Critter swims.

Point to the action word in each sentence below. Then find all of the action words in the story.

Little Critter dives.

Mom drives.

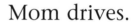

Little Sister eats.

Dad cooks.

# Answer Key

### page 19
### Matching Pictures

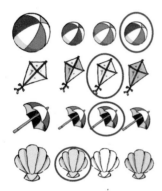

### page 20
### Color Words

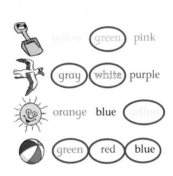

### page 21
### Understanding the Story

Besides Dad, who went to the beach with Little Critter?

What was one of the things Little Critter did with Little Sister?

What did Little Critter almost take home with him?

### page 22
### First Letter of a Word

 Kite

 ball

 pail

 fish

 seashell

 dune

### page 23
### Action Words

Little Critter dives.

Mom drives.

Little Sister eats.

Dad cooks.

From the story:

are going
spread
swim
build
play
pick up
take